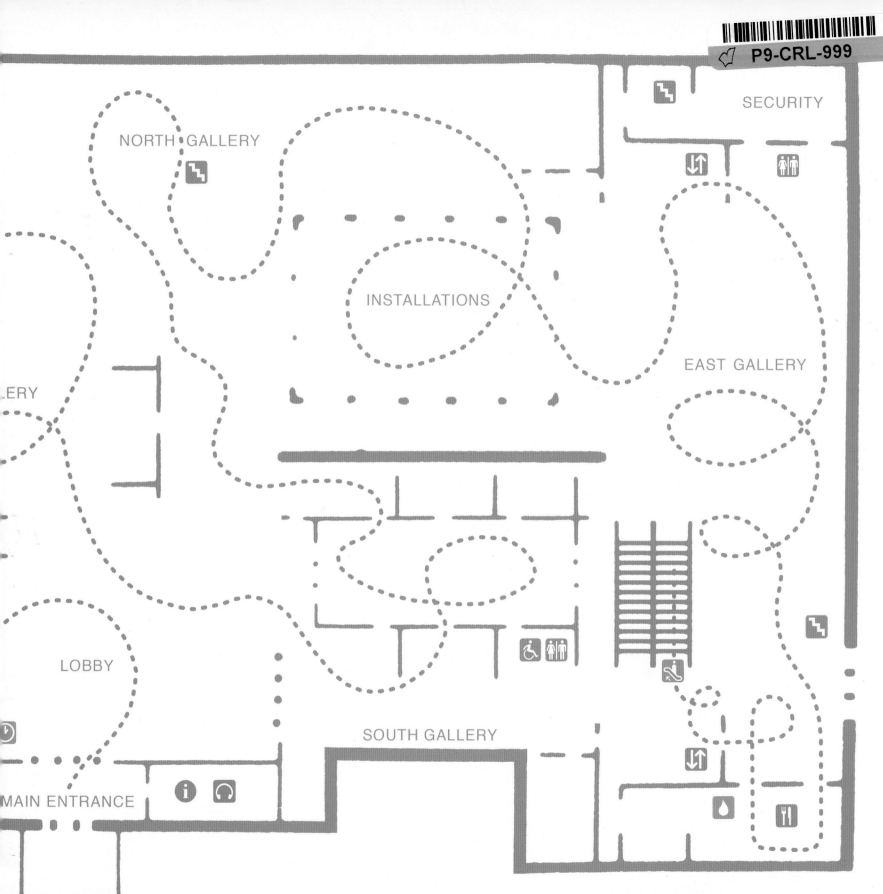

NORTH GALLERY

SECURITY

INSTALLATIONS

EAST GALLERY

ERY

LOBBY

SOUTH GALLERY

MAIN ENTRANCE

Meet Me at the Art Museum

A Whimsical Look Behind the Scenes

By David Goldin

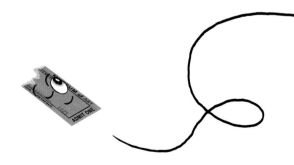

Abrams Books for Young Readers, New York

ARTIST'S NOTE

Creating this book was like building a real art museum. I had an idea, and then I had to find someone who could help make it happen: the publisher. I visited many museums for research. Then I became the director, making sure everything got done on time. I was the architect, figuring out the right environment and space to hold the artwork. I became a curator, trying to find a well-rounded collection of pieces to fill the rooms. I was the archivist, organizing all the images and keeping them in order. I was the conservator, cleaning up photos and correcting colors. There are so many art pieces I didn't include in this book . . . You'll have to go to a museum to see them for yourself. Welcome to my museum!

. . .

Cataloging-in-Publication Data has been applied for and may be obtained from the Library of Congress.

ISBN: 978-1-4197-0187-0

Published in 2012 by Abrams Books for Young Readers, an imprint of ABRAMS. All rights reserved. No portion of this book may be reproduced, stored in a retrieval system, or transmitted in any form or by any means, mechanical, electronic, photocopying, recording, or otherwise, without written permission from the publisher.

Printed and bound in China
10 9 8 7 6 5 4 3 2

Abrams Books for Young Readers are available at special discounts when purchased in quantity for premiums and promotions as well as fundraising or educational use. Special editions can also be created to specification. For details, contact specialsales@abramsbooks.com or the address below.

THE ART OF BOOKS SINCE 1949

115 West 18th Street
New York, NY 10011
www.abramsbooks.com

To Norbert and Miriam Porile,
who took me to the museum

Special thanks to Howard Reeves

When the museum closed for the night,
the cleaner did not see the ticket stub
lying on the granite floor.

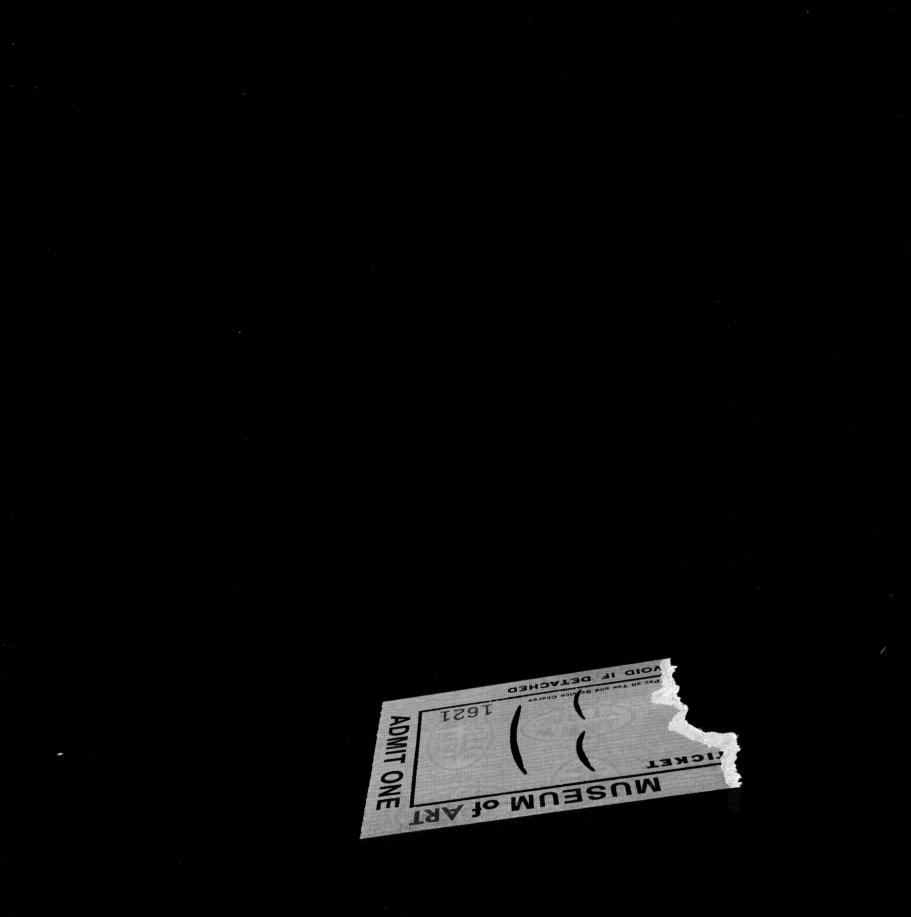

But someone else noticed him.
"Hello," said a friendly voice. "Who are you?"
"I'm Stub," the ticket said. "What is this place?"

"This is a museum, where some of the world's greatest treasures are kept on display. I'm Daisy, the docent's helper. The docent and I welcome visitors, take them on tours, and explain what is kept here."

"There are museums about science, art, sports—anything you can think of," said Daisy.

Stub wished he was a treasure so he could
live in such an awesome place.
"May I have a tour?" he asked.
"Sure," said Daisy. "I'll be your tour guide."

"Hey, pal. Got anything you want us
to hold for you while you walk around
the museum?" called a hat and glove.
"If you have a coat or backpack, you
can leave it at the coat check," said Daisy.
"Those guys live here in the lost and found."
"They're lucky to have a home," said Stub.

"This museum is big. How do you keep from getting lost?" he asked.

"See these signs?" explained Daisy. "They're all over the museum. They're designed to show you what's allowed and what's not, and where to find what you're looking for. It's called symbol signage—easy to understand, even if you can't read."

They walked past a huge room where new pieces of art were being delivered in carefully packaged crates. They then passed on to another large room.

CP-123

SCULPTURES WITHOUT LIMBS

SCULPTURES WITH LIMBS

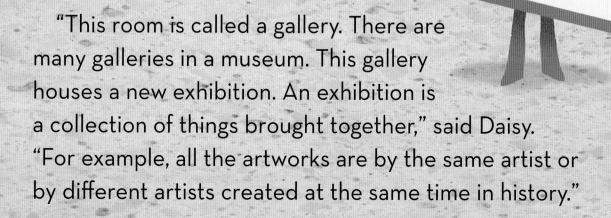

"This room is called a gallery. There are many galleries in a museum. This gallery houses a new exhibition. An exhibition is a collection of things brought together," said Daisy. "For example, all the artworks are by the same artist or by different artists created at the same time in history."

Stub saw paintings that made him think of sunny days . . .

. . . sculptures that made him curious . . .

. . . and others that made no sense at all but were fascinating in their own way.

"Who gets to choose what gets into a museum?" he asked.

"That's the curator's job," said Daisy. "The curator decides what is worthy of being in a museum. He or she is like a detective, making sure each piece is the real thing and not a copy."

Made in China

Stub couldn't resist reaching for a piece of art to see what it felt like. "Hands off," said Badge. "No touching allowed. Those are the rules of the museum. I'm the security guard, and I make sure they are followed."

"We use cameras and monitors so we can watch different galleries from the security room. Security lights help keep the treasures safe. Don't cross that red beam or an alarm will sound!"

17

"Other high-tech equipment is also used to keep precious objects safe," said Daisy. "It is the conservator's job to make sure the air is not too humid, not too dry.

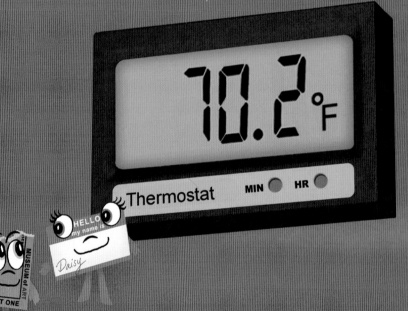

"They control the temperature. Not too hot, not too cold.

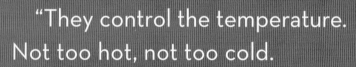

"They control the lights too. You can't have it too dark or too bright. Everything has to be just right. The conservator also fixes damaged objects in the museum's workshop."

Stub and his guide made their
way through the entire ground floor.
There was so much to see!

"Now is a good time for a break," said Daisy. "This is a café, where you can sit and rest your feet.

"The folks who live here will help you get a snack and a drink.

"You need to get your energy back, because there's another whole floor of treasures. You don't want to miss a single one!"

2nd
FLOOR

"What do you think so far?" asked Daisy.
"This place is amazing," said Stub. "I wish
I could stay forever."

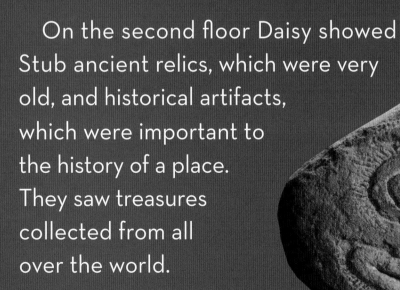

On the second floor Daisy showed
Stub ancient relics, which were very
old, and historical artifacts,
which were important to
the history of a place.
They saw treasures
collected from all
over the world.

Stub discovered . . .

ancient writing

sculptures of wood,
bronze, and stone

mobiles

paintings

costumes.

It was thrilling!

One day I'm gonna live
in a museum, thought Stub.

"When you have this much stuff, how do you keep
from losing things or getting them mixed up?" he asked.

On the computer screen:

Fang Tribal art mask.
Tribal art collection.

"An archivist catalogs each piece in the museum, keeping track of everything," said Daisy.

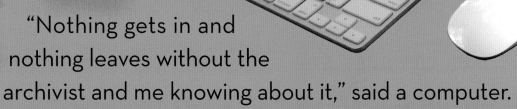

"Nothing gets in and nothing leaves without the archivist and me knowing about it," said a computer.

Down the hall, they passed the educator's room. "That's where all kinds of classes for kids and adults are taught."

. . . passed the director's office. "The director is in charge of the whole museum."

MUSEUM SHOP

. . . passed the museum shop. "Want to buy a souvenir?"

. . . and passed the library. "The librarian helps research subjects as well as collect and catalog books and other materials."

They toured the whole museum, except for one room. "That's where damaged treasures are fixed and restored," Daisy said, continuing to walk down the hall. But Stub paused to look inside.

"That's the tour," Daisy said. "Hey! Stub, where'd you go?"

Across the room a beautiful piece of artwork had caught Stub's eye. It was a collage.

Its colors and feeling of movement made him smile. He crept forward to get a closer look.

Suddenly a strong breeze caught hold of him!

He landed on the collage! It had just been given a fresh coat of varnish and was very, very sticky.

The next day the painting was hung in the main gallery. Stub had accidentally found the perfect home.

When you visit, perhaps you'll meet him *at the museum!*

Collage
The Dance (Inspired by Matisse)
by David Goldin 2011

Who's Who at the Museum

Many people work at an art museum. Some museums are very large and have a staff to match, while others are small or very specialized and have fewer employees. Here are some of the jobs that are found in an art museum. The responsibilities of a particular job differ from museum to museum.

The ARCHIVIST is in charge of cataloging and keeping track of information and objects relevant to the museum's collection. The "information and objects" can be photographs, films, video and sound recordings, and electronic data files as well as more traditional paper records, letters, and printed documents.

The CONSERVATOR cares for and restores the treasures that are kept in the museum. Both the storing and the exhibiting of items must be done in such a way as to keep them safe. For instance, strong light can cause colors to fade, moist air can make papers stick together, and dry air can make cloth and other materials fall apart. The conservator determines the appropriate climate-control for each object's preservation.

The CURATOR is an expert on a particular subject—for example, ancient Egypt or Impressionist painting—and is responsible for choosing and acquiring the pieces of art to be shown in the museum. The curator spends a great deal of time doing research and writing. Tracing the authenticity of an artifact—deciding whether it really was created by a particular person, is as old as someone claims it to be, and so on—involves real detective work. The curator is in charge of building the museum's own, or permanent, collection as well as overseeing pieces borrowed from other museums.

The DIRECTOR is in charge of the museum. He or she represents the museum to the public and works with the entire staff to make sure the museum runs smoothly.

The DOCENT welcomes visitors to the museum and leads tours of the museum's exhibits and collections. Docents tell the stories behind the treasures and answer questions. They are often volunteers who love art and enjoy talking about art with people.

The EDUCATOR provides learning tools about the museum for visiting schools and other groups. Educators often make public presentations, create lecture programs, and teach art classes.

The LIBRARIAN provides support to the curator, the conservator, and other staff members by helping to research and document the treasures as well as build a collection of books, digital information, and film and video relevant to the museum's collection.

The SECURITY GUARD and the MUSEUM SECURITY STAFF are responsible for the safety of the objects, the staff, and the visitors at the museum. They ensure that museum safety rules and also rules of etiquette are followed at all times. Security guards stand in the galleries to guard the objects and often can answer questions about the objects on display.

What's What at the Museum

An EXHIBITION is a collection of objects related in some manner and presented together.

A GALLERY is a room that houses an exhibition.

A MUSEUM is where treasures are kept for all to enjoy. Usually, a museum houses a particular type of treasure or treasures that are related to one another. Examples include a museum about sports, a museum of art, and a museum of human culture. A museum helps preserve the past, define the present, and educate for the future.

A TREASURE is anything that is worthy of being housed in a museum: artworks, photographs, stamps, dolls, clothes, artifacts, books . . . The list really is endless!

ART TITLES

The artworks shown in this book are currently located in the museum or collection referenced below or can be viewed on the Internet. All works referenced are left to right, top to bottom.

Pages 8–9: *Snap the Whip*, 1872, by Winslow Homer, Metropolitan Museum of Art, New York. *A Card Trick*, 1891–92, by John George Brown, Joslyn Art Museum, Omaha. *The Daughters of Edward Darley Boit*, 1882, by John Singer Sargent, Museum of Fine Art, Boston. **Page 12**: *Starry Night*, 1889, by Vincent van Gogh, Museum of Modern Art, New York. Native American clay pot, artist unknown. *Mona Lisa*, 1503–09, by Leonardo da Vinci, Musée du Louvre, Paris, France. *Peace*, 1820, by William Rush, Independence Seaport Museum, Philadelphia. **Page 13**: *Three Musicians*, 1921, by Pablo Picasso, Museum of Modern Art, New York. *Composition VII*, 1913, by Wassily Kandinsky, State Tretyakov Gallery, Moscow, Russia. *The City*, 1919, by Fernand Léger, The Tate, London. *Harlequin with Guitar*, 1919, by Juan Gris, Gallery Louise Leiris, Paris. *The Disks*, 1918–19, by Fernand Léger, Los Angeles County Museum of Art. (Two works on back wall by David Goldin.) *Roe Deer in the Forest*, 1914, by Franz Marc, Staatliche Kunsthalle, Germany. *Portrait of a Man with a Newspaper*, 1911–14, by André Derain, State Hermitage Museum, St. Petersburg, Russia. *Red Balloon*, 1922, by Paul Klee, The Solomon R. Guggenheim Museum, New York. *At the Cycle-Race Track*, 1912, by Jean Metzinger, Peggy Guggenheim Collection, Venice, Italy. **Page 14**: *A Sunday Afternoon on the Island of La Grande Jatte*, 1884–86, by Georges-Pierre Seurat, Art Institute of Chicago. *Wave*, 2011, by David Goldin, artist's collection. *Snowstorm*, 1842, by William Turner, The National Gallery, London. **Page 15**: *Luncheon of the Boating Party*, 1881, by Pierre-Auguste Renoir, The Phillips Collection, Washington, D.C. Roman mosaic, artist unknown, 2nd century BC–300 AD, private collection. Medieval manuscript, artist unknown, 12th–16th-century France, private collection. Ming Dynasty vase, 1368–1644, Metropolitan Museum of Art, New York. A replica of an ancient Egyptian papyrus, 2010, made in China. Paupau New Guinea mask, artist unknown. Ancient Greek statue, artist unknown. Ancient Greek head, artist unknown. Mayan sculpture, 250–900 AD, artist unknown. **Page 16**: *Composition with Red, Yellow, Blue and Black*, 1921, by Piet Mondrian, Gemeente Museum, the Hague, Netherlands. **Page 19**: *(Breezing Up) A Fair Wind*, 1873–1876, by Winslow Homer, National Gallery of Art, Washington, D.C. *Tulips in a Vase*, 1888–90, by Paul Cézanne, Norton Simon Museum, Pasadena, CA. *Fire Alarm*, 2009, by David Goldin, private collection. Ramses sitting, ancient Egypt, Metropolitan Museum of Art, New York. Buddha statue, artist unknown, David Goldin collection. *Doggie Treat*, photographer unknown, David Goldin collection. *Plane*, photographer unknown, David Goldin collection. **Page 22**: *I Ham I Am*, 2008, by David Goldin, artist's collection. *As American as Baseball and Apple Pie*, by Lenny Kislin, artist's collection. *Wink*, 2009, by David Goldin, artist's collection. *Flutist*, 2009, by David Goldin, artist's collection. *Volkswagon*, 2008, by David Goldin, artist's collection. *Fire Spirit*, 2010, by David Goldin, artist's collection. Greek Corinthian column, 400 BC, private collection. **Page 23**: Ancient Egyptian papyrus, date unknown. *Mercury Descending*, 2001, by David Goldin, artist's collection. *Colored Circles*, 2010, by Norm Magnusson, private collection. *Brown-Eyed Susan* (detail), 2010, by Norm Magnusson, private collection. *The Thinker*, 1902, by Auguste Rodin, Musée Rodin, Paris, France. Fashion illustrations, *McCall's* magazine, September 1920. *Promenade*, 2000, by Vladimir Bachinsky, artist's collection. *Costume Study*, 1998, by Vladimir Bachinsky, artist's collection. Ancient Greek statue, Woman with Cloak, artist unknown, terra-cotta, 4th–3rd century BC, private collection. *Waiting*, 1998, by Vladimir Bachinsky, artist's collection. Ancient Egyptian sarcophagus, unknown, private collection. *Colored Ovals*, 2010, by Norm Magnusson, private collection. **Page 24**: Fang Tribal masks, artists unknown, private collection. **Page 25**: Fang Tribal masks, artists unknown, private collection. **Page 26–27**: Medieval portrait of lady, artist unknown, private collection. *Jimmy's Run*, by David Goldin, artist's collection. *Jello Driver*, 2009, by David Goldin, artist's collection. *Comic Color*, 2010, by David Goldin, artist's collection. *Bottle Cap*, 2009, by David Goldin, artist's collection. *Bugler*, 1989, by David Goldin, artist's collection. **Page 29**: *The Dance*, 2011, by David Goldin, artist's collection. **Page 30**: *Pastoral*, 2007–2012, by Amy Cohen Banker, artist's collection and The Works Gallery, Madison Avenue, NYC. *Break Up*, 2011, by Nicole Eisenman, private collection. *Waterfall in Three Parts*, 2011, by Mariella Bisson, artist's collection. **Page 31**: *The Dance (Inspired by Matisse)*, 2011, by David Goldin, artist's collection.

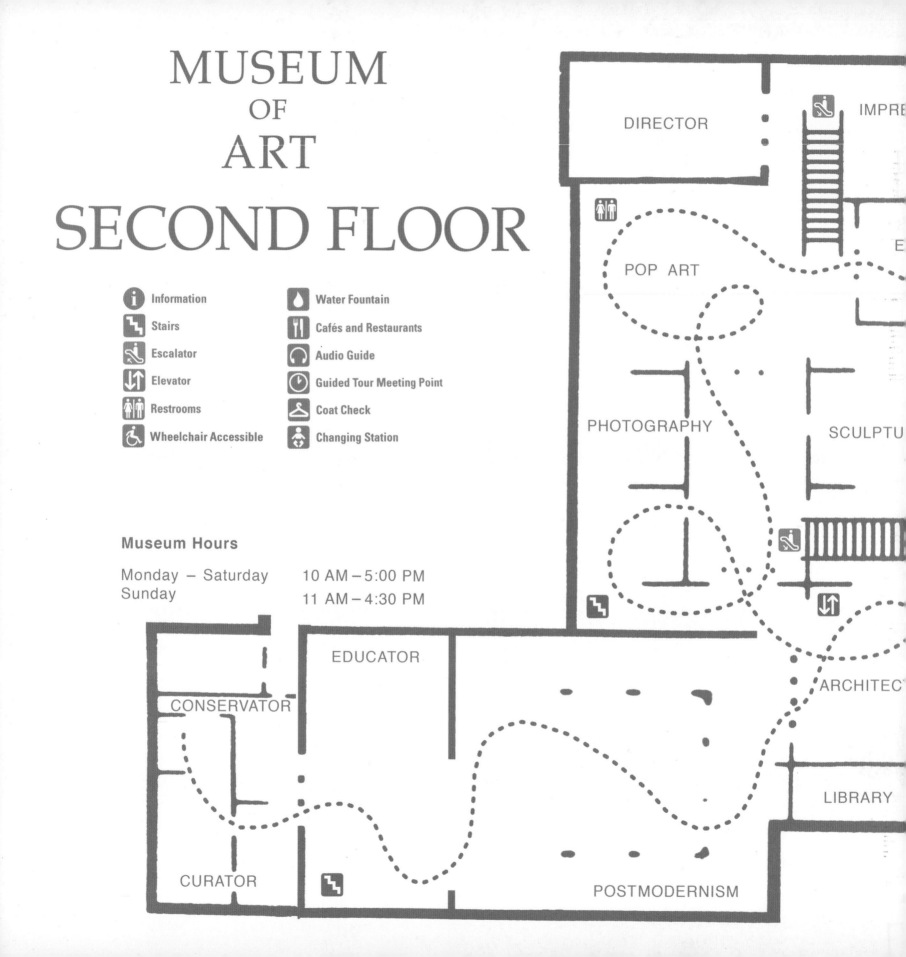

MUSEUM
OF
ART

SECOND FLOOR

Information

Stairs

Escalator

Elevator

Restrooms

Wheelchair Accessible

Water Fountain

Cafés and Restaurants

Audio Guide

Guided Tour Meeting Point

Coat Check

Changing Station

Museum Hours

Monday – Saturday   10 AM – 5:00 PM
Sunday   11 AM – 4:30 PM

DIRECTOR

IMPRE

POP ART

PHOTOGRAPHY

SCULPTU

E

EDUCATOR

CONSERVATOR

CURATOR

ARCHITEC

LIBRARY

POSTMODERNISM